W9-CDF-061

People do it, dogs do it, cars and trains too.
We **wave, wag, honk,** and even go **choo choo!**

hello YOU!

Sandra Magsamen

sourcebooks
wonderland

Howdy!
What's up?
Hey! and
How do you do?
There are a
gazillion
ways to say hello
to someone new!

Nobody knows anybody until they say **hi!** Give it a **chance,** just give it a **try!**

Even if you feel shy and don't know what to **say**, try a simple **wave**, it's a fun way to say...

It's never easy being the new kid in a new **place.** How about **welcoming** them with your smiling **face?**

If smiling
big and wide
isn't your thing,
try **humming** a
tune—you could
even **sing!**

And if singing just doesn't feel **right**, how about giving a **hug** with all your **might?**

If you think a **hug** feels a little bold, you could pick the biggest bunch of **flowers** you can **hold!**

But if that bunch of **flowers** makes you go "**achoo!**" try sitting at lunch with someone **new!**

If at lunch you prefer to just eat your **chocolate** cake, that's **ok.** At recess, try giving a **handshake!**

And if **hand** the right move, try **dance, shake,**

shakes aren't asking someone to or **groove!**

No matter how you say it, no matter your **way**, a little **hello** has the **power** to change someone's **day!**

We are all **one of a kind** with something special to **share.** Sometimes the most **awesome** friendships start with...

hey there!

This great big **world** of ours needs lots of love to keep it **strong**, and saying **hello** reminds us all that we are **loved** and ♡ we all **belong.**

Now you see what a simple **hello** can do!

So, it's time for everyone to **holler**...

hello
YOU!

Sandra Magsamen is a world-renowed artist, author, and designer whose products and ideas have touched millions of lives. Her books and stories are a heartfelt reminder that it's the people and moments in our lives that make life so wonderful!

Big heartfelt thanks to Karen Botti and Hannah Magsamen Barry. Their creativity and generous spirits are unique and valued gifts to me and the work we create in the studio.

Copyright © 2020 by Sandra Magsamen
Cover and internal design © 2020 by Sourcebooks
Text and illustrations © 2020 by Hanny Girl Productions, Inc. sandramagsamen.com

Sourcebooks and the colophon are registered trademarks of Sourcebooks.
All rights reserved.

Published by Sourcebooks Wonderland, an imprint of Sourcebooks Kids
P.O. Box 4410, Naperville, Illinois 60567-4410
(630) 961-3900
sourcebookskids.com

Library of Congress Cataloging-in-Publication Data is on file with the publisher.

Source of Production: 1010 Printing International, North Point, Hong Kong, China
Date of Production: April 2020
Run Number: 5018663

Printed and bound in China.
OGP 10 9 8 7 6 5 4 3 2

hellllll
llllll
llllll
llllll